WISE OWL'S STORY

BY ALISON UTTLEY

PICTURES BY MARGARET TEMPEST

Collins

First published in Great Britain by
William Collins Sons & Co in 1935
This edition published by
HarperCollins Publishers Ltd in 1993
Copyright © The Alison Uttley
Literary Property Trust 1986
Illustrations copyright
© The Estate of Margaret Tempest 1986
Copyright this arrangement
© William Collins Sons & Co Ltd 1986

Illustration on p. i by Mary Cooper
Alison Uttley's original story
has been abridged for this book.

A CIP catalogue record for this title
is available from the British Library.

ISBN: 0 00 194209 3

Printed and bound in Italy

This book is set in Goudy

Collins

An Imprint of HarperCollinsPublishers

FOREWORD

Of course you must understand that Grey Rabbit's home had no electric light or gas, and even the candles were made from pith of rushes dipped in wax from the wild bees' nests, which Squirrel found. Water there was in plenty, but it did not come from a tap. It flowed from a spring outside, which rose up from the ground and went to a brook. Grey Rabbit cooked on a fire, but it was a wood fire, there was no coal in that part of the country. Tea did not come from India, but from a little herb known very well to country people, who once dried it and used it in their cottage homes. Bread was baked from wheat ears, ground fine, and Hare and Grey Rabbit gleaned in the cornfields to get the wheat.

The doormats were plaited rushes, like country-made mats, and cushions were stuffed with wool gathered from the hedges where sheep pushed through the thorns. As for the looking-glass, Grey Rabbit found the glass, dropped from a lady's handbag, and Mole made a frame for it. Usually the animals gazed at themselves in the still pools as so many country children have done. The country ways of Grey Rabbit were the country ways known to the author.

Wise Owl lived in the hollow oak tree in the middle of the wood. Anyone could see it was Wise Owl's house, for a little silver bell with an eagle on it, and curly lines like a shell round its edges, hung beside the front door. There were windows high up in the tree, hidden in the rough bark, and a wisp of blue smoke came out of the chimney among the leaves, when Owl was at home.

Sometimes bits of the tree fell into the soup when Owl was cooking, but he was too wise a bird to mind.

The house was very old and very untidy. Dust and dirt of ages filled the rooms, and cobwebs hung in festoons from the ceiling. There were little attics and store-rooms all over the tree, filled with lumber and old wood and spiders. Wise Owl never went into these rooms, for he kept to his kitchen, his bedroom, and his study.

In the bedroom there was a little four-poster, with a small carved owl perched on each bed-post, and on it lay a goose-feather bed. In the kitchen was a frying-pan, but in the study were all Owl's books of wisdom.

One evening, just as dusk fell, Owl yawned and got down from his easy-chair, where he had been dozing. He sniffed at the cool air which came through the window. The wind had changed, and there was a strange rippling motion which he felt at once in his feathers.

"A storm's brewing somewhere," said he to himself. "There will be a gale tonight. I must shut the windows before I go out, or my books will get wet."

That night the wind whirled through the wood in a fury. It tossed the trees and snapped the branches. It rattled and banged at the doors and windows of all the little houses in the fields and hedgerows.

Mole, in his underground house, knew nothing of the storm, but Mrs Hedgehog awoke her husband in the cottage close by.

"There's a crash!" said she. "Get up, Hedgehog, and see what's the matter. I believe our house has blown down."

Old Hedgehog crawled sleepily to the window, and stared out. On the ground under the hedge was a little hollow chimney, rolling about among the leaves.

"Th' chimbley's come off," said he. "It was a great noise for our little chimbley."

"What shall we do? Suppose the house blows away?" cried Mrs Hedgehog.

"Our house is safe enough, wife," said Hedgehog. "It's the big things that goes in a storm. Church steeples, and great trees, not tiddly houses like ours." He climbed back to bed and fell asleep in spite of Mrs Hedgehog's protests.

When Wise Owl's hunting was over, he tried to fly back to his tree, but it wasn't there!

"Am I bewitched?" said he. "Have I come to the wrong wood?" Then he looked down to the ground, and he saw the oak tree stretched out like a fallen giant. The door was broken off, books lay scattered on the grass, and the silver bell had gone.

"Oh woe! Woe is me!" cried the Owl. "Too-whit! Too-whoo! What shall I do?"

His great wisdom deserted him, and he was just a lonely, unhappy owl, very wet and very tired, with no home to rest in.

The next morning the gale dropped, but the rain poured down. Little Grey Rabbit could hear the patter of the drops on the roof as she dressed, and she looked from her window at a drenched world.

"I wonder what that crash was I heard in the night," said she to herself. "I'll just slip out while the others are asleep. I want to wear my new goloshes."

She brought out her shiny goloshes from the hole under the stairs. She slipped a cloak over her shoulders and ran out in the wet, down the path to the wood.

"My feet are quite dry!" she exclaimed, as she paddled through a pool.

When she got near Wise Owl's house, she saw the fallen tree and the broken door and all the tumbled wet books.

"Oh! Poor Wise Owl! What will he do with no home!" she cried, and she gathered up some of the books, and put them under the tree for shelter.

She looked round for Wise Owl, but he was nowhere to be seen, so she hurried back with her sad news.

"We must all *do* something," said Hare, as he ate his porridge.

"Yes, let's *do* something really useful," said Squirrel.

"Should we invite him here as our guest until he finds another house?" asked Grey Rabbit.

"Here?" exclaimed Hare, puckering up his face. "In this house, Grey Rabbit? Are you mad?"

"No, it wouldn't do," agreed Grey Rabbit. "He must have a house of his own."

There was silence for a moment, and then Grey Rabbit said, "Suppose we go out and look for one for him."

"Can't he do that himself?" grumbled Squirrel.

"He doesn't like the daylight, you know, and at night he is too busy," said Grey Rabbit. "We will wait till the rain stops, and then we will take sandwiches and spend the day house-hunting!"

"Sandwiches? Splendid!" cried Hare. "I love house-hunting!" He ran to the door and looked out.

"There's a rainbow in the sky, Grey Rabbit. We can go quite soon."

The three animals set out on their expedition through the wood, but although they looked to the right and the left, high up and low down, they couldn't find a hollow tree.

They took their sandwiches out of their pockets and sat down to eat them near the fallen tree. Grey Rabbit fished the little dictionary out of the pool and wiped it on her handkerchief. Squirrel found a book of nursery songs in a briar bush. Hare picked up a history book, but that was quite dry.

"I wonder where Wise Owl is," said Grey Rabbit, and she peeped through the door into the dusty rooms.

"Let us all go different ways," said Squirrel. "Then if we haven't found a house by teatime, we will go home."

Hare tossed a straw in the air, to see which way he should go, and then he set off down an inviting little green path. He soon found himself out of the wood, in a wet green meadow. There in the grass grew round, white satiny knobs.

"Mushrooms!" he cried, and he filled his pockets. He forgot all about Wise Owl's house as he wandered about the field. At the gate he met an elderly rabbit leaning on a crutch, and they stood talking.

"Such a wind! It blew the garden gate off its hinges," said the rabbit, "and I hobbled in for my breakfast."

"Is the gate still down?" asked Hare.

"Oh yes. There's plenty left," replied the rabbit. Hare thanked him, gave him a pawful of mushrooms, and then ran with his long legs across the fields to the farm garden.

Squirrel started off along a little path in the opposite direction, and came to a mountain ash. Up she ran, and rubbed her cheeks against the scarlet berries. She picked a bunch, and threaded them on a grass. Then she hung them round her neck, and gazed at herself in a pool of rain water.

"Scarlet suits me," said she, and she certainly looked very pretty with her necklace.

A silver birch stood in her path, and she stood before the lovely white tree, with its tiny pointed leaves. She stripped off a piece of the bark and wound it round her paws. Then she ran up the tree and sported herself on the delicate sprays of green.

Little Grey Rabbit ran along the path to the West, looking to right and left for a hollow tree. She dodged in and out, sniffing and searching, and she marked each tree with a tiny white cross, so that none should be overlooked. She worked so hard, she did not notice that the afternoon had passed, and evening was approaching. She tapped the trees, and marked them, moving farther and farther from home, until at last she heard the sound she had been listening for all day.

She stopped in front of a great beech tree and tapped again. It was hollow!

Here was a house for Wise Owl! She ran round the trunk and pulled away the brambles and leaves which concealed the opening. Then, rather frightened, she went inside.

There was a splendid empty house! It was rather damp of course, but a little fire would soon dry it. There were three rooms, and lots of attics, and shelves all round the walls. It was just right for Wise Owl.

She went to the door and looked out. The moon was rising behind the hill, and a soft golden glow spread over the wood. She didn't know where she was, and there was nothing to be done, except to stay there all night. She picked up a tiny glow-worm and carried it in with her. She climbed on to a rough shelf, made herself as small as possible, and fell asleep, with the glow-worm shining like a little night-light.

When Hare went home, he found Squirrel sitting rocking herself backwards and forwards.

"Where is Little Grey Rabbit?" asked Hare. "Hasn't she come home yet?"

"No, she probably met Wise Owl, and they talked about tails and bells and hollow trees," said Squirrel.

Hare put a lighted candle in the window and then he stood at the door and called "Coo-ee. Coo-ee."

Wise Owl came out of the wood-shed, "Did you call?" he asked coolly.

"We've lost Grey Rabbit," explained Hare. "She is looking for a house for you."

"A house for me?" echoed Wise Owl. "I am going to live in your wood-shed."

He stepped into the house and snapped up all the mushrooms and hot buttered toast which lay ready for supper.

"I'd better go off and find Grey Rabbit," said Wise Owl. "You stay here, and wait up for her."

Hare mopped his brow.

"Whew!" he cried. "I did feel nervous. I never thought I should live to see the day when an Owl would come into the kitchen and eat my supper before my very eyes!"

Wise Owl flew over the woods, calling, but either the tree was too thick or Grey Rabbit was too fast asleep, she never heard his voice, and he had to return without her.

"She's lost!" he said huskily. "Little Grey Rabbit's gone. I asked the stoat, and several other people, but no one had seen her."

Hare and Squirrel were very much alarmed, for Wise Owl was a famous finder of lost animals.

"I'm going to sleep now," said he. "Don't disturb me. You two must go out and look for her. The morning's here, and Hedgehog the milkman is starting on his rounds. No dilly-dallying! Off you go to look for your companion."

"He orders us about as if he lived here," complained Squirrel. "Oh, I do wish Grey Rabbit would come back!"

There was a sound outside, the door was pushed open, and in came little Grey Rabbit, looking as fresh as a daisy. She had washed in a stream, and brushed her hair with a teasel brush.

"Wherever have you been?" cried Hare. "We were just going to look for you. Owl was hunting for you all night."

Little Grey Rabbit turned pale.

"To find you, not to eat you," said Hare crossly.

"I am so sorry," said Grey Rabbit humbly. "I got lost. But I found a home for Owl!"

"Thank goodness," exclaimed Hare. "Is it a nice house, Grey Rabbit? Owl is in the wood-shed and he won't go away."

"Couldn't we spring-clean it for him, whilst he is asleep, and put his books inside, and then he will want to go?" asked Squirrel.

"Oh yes!" cried Grey Rabbit.

Then they took buckets and mops and scrubbing brushes and soap, and walked off to the wood.

Grey Rabbit led them to a beautiful beech tree, with golden brown leaves spreading in a tent overhead.

"It's a fine tree," said Hare, "but where is the door?" Grey Rabbit pointed out the small hole near the ground.

"Owl won't want to fly down to the earth when he comes home," objected Hare. "I don't think he will change from the wood-shed."

Then he added hurriedly, "Excuse me a moment. I've forgotten something. I must run home," and away he went.

Squirrel and Grey Rabbit filled their buckets from the pool near, and they scrubbed and mopped the floors and walls and ceilings.

They beeswaxed the shelves, and lined them with fresh beech-leaves.

"Owl will be able to keep all his books here," said Squirrel. "There's a place for his blotting-paper, and his pen and ink, and –"

"Tape measure and thimble," interrupted Hare, coming in carrying a saw.

"What's that for?" asked Squirrel.

"It's a saw to saw things," said Hare. "Do you imagine that Wise Owl would live here with that door? Why, he couldn't get through it without crawling! So I'm going to make a door, high up, so that he can fly in!"

He climbed up the steep stairs, and cut a neat door in the tree.

"A nice airy house with every modern convenience," said he proudly, as he stepped backwards to view his work, but he trod on the soap and fell downstairs to the bottom of the tree.

"The proper place to keep soap is the larder, so put it there," cried he, rubbing his head, and calling up to Squirrel. "Never leave soap on the stairs, Squirrel." So Squirrel placed it on the larder shelf.

The three animals went to the oak tree and collected the books, which were now dry with the wind and the sun. They carried them across to the new house, and arranged them on the shelves.

They returned for Owl's rush-bottomed chair, and three-legged stool, his feather-bed and frying-pan. Hare found the sealing-wax, and Squirrel the candlestick, and little Grey Rabbit found his night-cap dangling in the nettles, but nowhere could they see the little silver bell.

"Moley's bell," sighed little Grey Rabbit. "It was such a beautiful bell, and it saved my tail. I do hope it will turn up."

The house was finished and they stood in the grass staring up and admiring the shiny grey trunk of the tree, and the sloping boughs with the little door hidden among them, when Hedgehog walked up.

"Hello!" said he. "I've just found Owl's bell. I was walking along the path through the wood, looking for a new chimbley for our house, when I heard a tinkly tinkle, and there was a mouse playing with Owl's bell!"

"A bold mouse!" said Hare. "Luckily for him, Owl is asleep in our wood-shed."

He explained the disasters of the night of the storm.

Little Grey Rabbit took the silver bell and examined it. It was none the worse but she rubbed it, and polished it. Then Squirrel ran up the tree and hung it at the side of Owl's front door, and the four walked back to the little house at the edge of the wood.

"Wake up, Wise Owl," they cried, "Wake up. There's a new house for you in the wood."

"Don't want a new house," muttered Wise Owl sleepily. "Go away."

"Your books are on the shelves," said Hare.

"Your night-cap is on the bed," said Grey Rabbit.

"Your bell's a-tinkling by the front door," said Hedgehog.

Wise Owl came out and blinked at them.

"Did you say you had put my tree up again?" he asked.

"No. We've found another, a better one," said Little Grey Rabbit.

Without another word Wise Owl flew off, flapping silently away in the daylight, never heeding the crowd of small birds which followed after. They twittered and cried, but Owl saw the silver bell, and he pushed open the door. He walked upstairs, one step at a time, and he looked in all the cupboards and on the shelves.

"I must give a present each to the Squirrel, the Hare and the Little Grey Rabbit. They've certainly done me a good turn."

He searched in his treasure box, which was buried deep in the brown leaf-mould of the wood, and he took them – what do you think?

A tiny basket, carved out of a cherry stone; a sailing boat, made from half a walnut-shell; a little beech-tree growing out of a beech-nut! Now can you guess which had which?